The Treehou~

Tessy Braun

"And Hansel said to Gretel: 'Let us drop these breadcrumbs so that together we find our way home. Because losing your way would be the most cruel of things"

~ **Hansel and Gretel**

CONTENTS

ACKNOWLEDGMENTS

A story inspired by my own stay in a treehouse with my lovely boyfriend, David.

Thank you to those who gave me feedback during the creation of this short story, in particular my mum, Billy and Sarah-Louise.

PROLOGUE

"Grandma, tell me the story again," begged the little girl who was finally tucked up in her bed. Grandma glanced at the clock noting that at nearly nine pm, it was well past the little girl's bedtime. She stroked her long straw-coloured hair and kissed her on the forehead.

"I think that's just about enough, Caroline. I don't want you to have bad dreams tonight."

She pursed her lips, "I won't!" said the little girl quite insistently. "I'm *not* scared of the woodlands, Grandma!"

Grandma smiled, "I know, you're a *very* brave girl, but dreams can be funny things, and it's getting rather late now, you should be fast asleep."

"Grandma, tell me about the lights again, that part isn't scary at all!"

The old lady sighed, "Alright, but after that, you *must* sleep." The child nodded in agreement.

"Well, it all began when night had fallen. The wind rustled through the leaves, whistling here and there, and if you closed your eyes and listened very carefully you may well hear…"

Tessy Braun

THE CALL OF THE WILD

Caz and Kenny paused to drink some water. Their bag straps tugged on their sun kissed shoulders, and after walking three miles in the sweltering sunshine they were desperate to finally arrive at the treehouse.

Kenny wiped the sweat from his brow, "Oh geez, I wish we had been able to drive," he guzzled more water down before wiping his mouth. Caz took his water bottle and replaced it in his rucksack pocket.

"Well, it *is* an eco-break darling, and cars are strictly forbidden."

Despite her relaxed outlook, Caz secretly wondered what on Earth had possessed her to book two nights in an off grid self-sufficient treehouse in the middle of nowhere. She shook her head, 'roughing it' had never been her 'thing', and the thought of using a composting toilet still repulsed her, even with six months to make peace with the idea. Yet something had attracted her to the hand crafted get-away which hung from the trees in the midst of a Wiltshire forest. Could it have been the call of the wild within her? Perhaps the desire to truly get away from technology and the stress of modern life? She had to admit that the thought of switching her phone off, thereby disconnecting from her material troubles had sounded blissful at the time.

They continued their way until the unnamed road narrowed into a smaller path lined thickly with long grass and nettles.

Caz pursed her lips, "Is this *definitely* the right way, Kenny?"

He sighed, now feeling a little frustrated with the relentless heat and the weight of the bags he was carrying, (Kenny never travelled light).

"You're the one that planned this trip Caz - *you tell me!*"

Caz laughed, determined not to let his bad mood dampen her spirits. "Come on, don't get cross."

He huffed, "Next time you book something for my birthday, please run it past me *first*, okay?"

Dismissing his negativity, she giggled, "You'll love it when you get there, you'll see!"

Caz chuckled to herself, poor Kenny had not had the best of nights. He must have had a nightmare, for Caz had found him on the landing floor in the small hours, yet he insisted he never left the bedroom intentionally.

Caz took a deep breath. She couldn't quite believe that she was feeling so casual about staying in the treehouse. A treehouse that would no doubt be complete with creepy crawlies. Not only that, but the facilities included the use of a bucket shower and a compost loo. There was no chambermaid to make the bed either. It wasn't quite the five-star rating she had been used to in the past. In fact, 'eco' breaks weren't really up her street at all, but something had drawn her to the treehouse and if she were honest, she could still feel its force calling her right there and then. She had hoped that Kenny would like it too, after all he loved stargazing and Caz had thought the location would be perfect for observing the night sky. Though, if truth be told Kenny was rather used to his creature comforts and there was some doubt in her mind as to whether 'slumming it' would be something he could learn to love.

Kenny had been out with his mates last night for his monthly curry club meal and he was still suffering from a very sore head. Caz could still smell the alcohol on his breath, so no wonder he was a little irritable, *he'll soon settle down once we find the place*, she thought.

After consulting the hand drawn map that the travel agent had provided, the consensus was to take the narrowing path to the right of the fork ahead, and it wasn't long before they saw a burgundy canopy in the vegetation upfront.

"Look, that must be the fire pit area!" Caz exclaimed, "The Treehouse must be *really* close!" Kenny was a few metres ahead and turning to his left he stopped and let out a half sigh, half laugh, "We're here, at long *bloody* last!"

Caz also turned to face the edge of the copse and at first couldn't see anything at all. "Look!" said Kenny pointing up into the forest. Then she saw it. Up the hill a short distance, there was a balcony high up in the treetops, he was right, they had arrived.

Tessy Braun

WE WON'T BE NEEDING THOSE BLANKETS

They trudged up some shallow log steps, which gave way to a precarious slope. Low and behold before them stood the treehouse in all its glory. They lifted their heads up to take it all in. It was hauntingly beautiful and even though they had seen pictures on the internet, the true image held far more of an impact. They stood there for a moment, admiring the craftsmanship, it was just marvellous in all manner of ways.

A tingle ran down Caz's spine, and her heart felt like it skipped a beat as a peculiar feeling bubbled inside her and a sense of nostalgia took hold. The feeling of Deja vu was extraordinary, even though she had never been there before.

"What do you think, Kenny?" She shivered despite the sunshine, as they reached the foot of the fluted walkway with a sense of trepidation. The treehouse was built upon a platform in the red cedar trees, and the walkway flexed as they made their way up.

The treehouse certainly had a unique charm. As they reached the platform, they were delighted to find a table with candles and lanterns, and to the side, a hammock that was calling Kenny's name.

To the right of the table they found the sleeping pod, containing no more than a double bed. The artistry was simply beautiful with little windows and wooden beams, and every little detail was thought of. Kenny was particularly impressed with the little hooks for head lamps and torches on the ceiling. However, Caz was afraid to look *too* closely in fear of what she may find lurking in the corners of the woodwork. She hoped that she would not be sharing her bed with any spiders that night.

Kenny called from the other side of the platform, "Check this out, Caz!" He pulled a thick heavy curtain which hung between two wooden panels to reveal a tiny room with two facing seats. The board game "Scrabble" was on the drop-down table between them, and there was a shelf in the room with two half burned candles.

"The confessional," remarked Caz, "Wow, this place is well thought out," she said, noting the two tartan blankets and the box of candles under one of the seats.

"I'm glad it's summer and we won't be needing those blankets," said Kenny as he unzipped his rucksack to retrieve his nerdy science book. Before Caz had a chance to say 'Huntsford Copse Treehouse', Kenny was in the hammock with a cheeky smile. That being said, before long the book was resting on his nose and Caz could just about make out a muffled snore coming from underneath.

A BUCKET IN THE TREE

Caz left him to relax while she went back to the ground level to put their food away. The kitchen was within twenty metres of the treehouse and consisted of a wooden hut with two gas hobs and a gas-powered fridge. In addition, there was a big box of mismatched crockery for the guests to make use of.

A few more metres passed the kitchen area, Caz located the shower, which was nothing more than a bucket in one of the smaller trees. She touched the back of her neck; it was so sweaty from the journey and she longed to freshen up. It would mean heating up the water in the giant cast iron kettle and pouring the water into the bucket, but she just knew it would be worth it. She let down her straw-coloured hair from her ponytail, and that in itself was a relief as it had been so tightly secured.

She used the rope to hoist the bucket above her head and secured the rope loop to the supporting plank of wood. *Easy*! She thought.

To her delight, the sun was still remarkably warm when she slipped off her dress and stepped underneath the makeshift shower head. The water dribbled out with little force, but it was refreshing, nonetheless. Caz enjoyed the sensation of the water, taking relish in the bubbles from her shower gel, (which would probably be the only snippet of luxury she would experience that weekend.)

As she lathered her hair, she heard the gentle rush of the wind through the leaves and the distant low of cattle. The sounds of nature were reassuring and quite pleasing to the ear. She continued to wash, but all of a sudden what she was listening to changed, and now to her astonishment a more tuneful sound was heard. It began softly, like a smooth melody drifting through the air. The dulcet tones sounded most like those of a woman, though she couldn't quite place it. Whatever the sound was, it was hypnotising. A pretty murmur almost unworldly, and Caz found herself gently humming along to it, not for one moment perturbed.

Then, abruptly, a wave of uncertainty broke over her, as if she were plummeting back down to reality after a strange dream. She had the sense that someone's eyes were upon her, "*Who's there*!?" she shouted out. She grabbed her towel from the nearby tree branch and peeked over the hessian shower curtain. Her eyes darted around the nearby bushes and up into the forest. She could still very much hear the strange murmur, but it was now ever so slowly fading.

Caz tried to think logically. Could it have been a car stereo blaring out from miles away, or perhaps someone on a bicycle with one of those portable stereos in their backpack? She didn't know, but what she did know, was that she felt drained and couldn't shake off the mysterious singing that she had heard echoing through the woods. With no further delay she hurriedly made her way back to the treehouse to tell Kenny.

Her thighs burned as she clambered up the hill, and she didn't manage the slope very well at all in flip flops, having to momentarily stop to flick the bark away from her toes.

"Kenny!" She yelled, but the only reply was the squawk of a crow. *Typical*, she thought, he's still asleep. She clambered up the fluted walkway clutching her clothes and holding the towel tightly around her.

"Kenny!" She cried again, but he wasn't in the hammock. *Where* was he!? He hadn't gone to bed, surely? Caz peaked into the sleeping pod, but Kenny wasn't in there either.

On closer inspection of the hammock Caz concluded that wherever he was he had left in a hurry. He had not worn his sliders for they were strewn by the side of the hammock along with his nerdy book and sunglasses. Perhaps he had gone to the loo, thought Caz.

"Kenny!" she hollered, with increasing concern. *This wasn't funny.* Despite her panic she almost expected Kenny to jump out at her from behind a branch, but he didn't.

The leaves rustled, and a peculiar whispering sound emanated from the woodland. It engulfed her entirely, so much so she could almost feel the strange whispers tickling her skin. She dropped her belongings on the deck, threw some clothes on, laced up her trainers and ran back down to the ground level once more. Reaching the kitchen, she saw no sign of Kenny. She passed the toilet, and finally arrived at the fire pit, but Kenny was nowhere to be seen. Caz held her mobile phone up towards the heavens - *dammit, no signal* - when they said this place was off the grid, they sure meant *off the grid*!

In a state of panic, she sat down on one of the wooden benches by the firepit and stared out into the Wiltshire countryside. If this was some kind of sick joke, Kenny was going to get it in the neck later.

Caz's attention was drawn to a helicopter soaring in the sky above, creating an awful racket in the otherwise peaceful countryside. It was one of those double-bladed ones, a chinook, if Caz recalled correctly, (Kenny would have known for sure).

With no sign of Kenny, Caz rapidly began to lose her cool, becoming more unnerved by the second. The strange noises and sensations she was experiencing were not helping one bit. Suddenly she heard heavy panting and footsteps from the direction of the trees. Caz jumped. She didn't know what to expect, or from what direction, whatever it was, was coming from. Should she try to hide, or run? It all happened at such speed, and just a millisecond after she made the decision to run, the footsteps were right behind her back and a heavy hand landed on her right shoulder. She screamed a truly awful scream and spun around.

"Caz! It's me!"

She turned; Kenny stood there drained of all colour as if he had seen a ghost. "Kenny! Where on earth have you been?!"

Kenny's face was a picture of pure confusion, "I, I don't know, I fell asleep, and I was dreaming. It was a really vivid one, like it wasn't a dream at all," he paused, and took a deep breath. "A woman came to me while I was lying in the hammock, she was very pretty, I remember that." he said. Caz rolled her eyes, "*and*" she pressed.

"She was singing," he went on, trying to recall what he had seen in his dream.

Caz gasped! "*What?!*"

"Yes, she was singing, and she had the most beautiful enchanting voice, Caz." Caz's jaw hung open in disbelief for she too had heard the beautiful singing, but she hadn't been asleep. She pinched herself to check if she was actually awake right there and then. "Ow!" she squeaked, (she was very much awake).

"*It was so real, Caz*. The woman held out her hand and led me deep into the forest, to one of those tall red cedar trees."

"Go on," said Caz, intrigued and bemused by his somewhat familiar story.

"Well, it's all a bit blurry now, but what I do remember is that with one hand she beckoned me to the tree, closer and closer, and she kind of moved *into* the tree. With the other hand, she pulled me towards her, still singing a strange kind of lullaby, it was all extremely hypnotising."

"And then?!"

"And then, there was a terrifying growl, or a roar, like a lion or something, it was the strangest dream Caz, but the weird thing is when I woke up, I wasn't in the hammock. I was by the stump of a tree, and I didn't have my sliders on, no idea how I got there, I must have sleep-walked." The two of them hugged.

"Yes, my darling, you must have sleep-walked."

Tessy Braun

THREE WHISTLES

     While Kenny caught his breath, for some reason Caz began to think back to her dear old grandma, who was sadly not with them anymore. Caz couldn't remember exactly what had happened, but one day when she was still only a little girl, her grandma had disappeared. One day she was there, and the next, well, she wasn't. She thought back to the stories that her grandma used to tell her when she was little. Caz hadn't cast her mind back to them for many years. They seem to have been naturally suppressed after her beloved grandmother left so suddenly which caused Caz much distress and sadness. Back then Caz's imagination would be filled with Woodland Fae, Tree Nymphs, and other mythical creatures of the woodlands.

     Since being in the forest this weekend, her memories had been re-ignited, and it was then she began to realise why this location seemed so familiar. It really was just how her grandma had described it in the stories - the beautiful singing Nymph, the enchanting music, the mysterious red cedar trees. Yet that was all she could remember from those tales, it was after all a good thirty-five years ago, and she hadn't thought of them since. After some consideration, she decided not to tell Kenny about her experience in the shower. She didn't want to freak him out any more than he already was. She *was* of course a little freaked out herself, but she was *sure* that there would be a logical explanation to all the strange goings on. The music was just a distant car stereo, Kenny heard it too, while he was sleeping, nothing more, nothing less. She didn't want to spoil the weekend break, and she decided it was best if they both tried to relax and enjoy the time together instead. After all they were both ravenous, and it had already past six o clock.

Kenny lit the grill and Caz prepared a bowl with some Doritos and salsa dip. She filled another with salad, and they were both looking forward to a tasty tea.

At various occasions throughout the evening both Caz and Kenny had to pop back to the treehouse to retrieve something they had left or go to the toilet. For a bit of fun, they devised a signal to let the other know they had reached the destination safely. The signal consisted of three short whistles. Although it was only a bit of a joke to start with, they both found it reassuring to hear the signal being repeated by the other. By now Caz had had a few cans of premixed gin and tonic spritzer and was feeling a little lightheaded. She giggled; *this wasn't so bad after all!*

"Honestly, Caz, I take it all back," Kenny put his arm around her and gave her a gentle squeeze. "This is a great little adventure, *thank you.*"

She grinned, and then kissed him on the lips.

"I love you Kenny Kempton."

The sun set over the Wiltshire hills, lighting the sky up in a soft orange hue. It had been an enjoyable evening. They had sat at the foot of the forest where the landscape opened up into a field, and all the time they had been accompanied by a farmer in his tractor harvesting in the far off distance; it had been somewhat comforting.

Twilight soon morphed into the dead of night and the pair huddled together under a blanket of stars.

"Let's go back to the treehouse," suggested Kenny, "we can sit outside on the deck and light some candles."

Caz agreed wholeheartedly, it was starting to feel a little creepy with so much dark space around them. The treehouse would be much cosier. She quickly nipped into the kitchen to grab a knife to cut the birthday cake she had brought with her for Kenny. He didn't know about it yet, she thought it would be a nice surprise. When she had gone back to the treehouse earlier, she had left it in a tin on the table, ready for his return.

As they walked hand in hand up the slope small twigs snapped beneath their feet, and Caz jumped when the hoot of an owl came from nowhere. The atmosphere had certainly begun to shift now that the night had fallen.

She stopped to catch her breath and rested her hand upon what she thought was a branch of a tree, but it was cold to the touch and completely rigid.

"Kenny, shine your phone torch down here a minute, babe,"

The dim beam revealed a metal post and not a branch at all, as Caz had suspected. As the light rolled over the structure, they wondered why they hadn't noticed it in the daylight. Caz gasped as she clocked the thick chain attached to the post. They followed the chain, which was as thick as Kenny's arm, but it came to an end after a metre or so.

"What was that for!?" asked Kenny.

"I don't know…" said Caz, thinking back to the 'dream' Kenny had and the monstrous growl he had mentioned. Had something escaped into the forest that afternoon? Caz was beginning to wonder why she had not told Kenny that she had also heard the strange singing in the woods, and that his dream may not have been a dream after all.

She clutched Kenny's hand perhaps a little too tightly. "Owww!" he yelped.

She rubbed it, "Sorry darling."

Tessy Braun

A FOX, OR SOMETHING

The pair made themselves comfortable up on the deck, and the soft glow of the candles alleviated any feelings of anxiety. Kenny cracked open another cider, before noticing the cake tin on the table. "Happy belated birthday darling!" she handed him the knife, "I know it was back in February, but this weekend was to celebrate you turning forty, go on cut us a slice!"

After enjoying the cake, they started to quiz each other, which was a pastime they both found enjoyable. Though without an internet signal they were quickly running out of questions to ask each other when Caz suddenly remembered, "I know, wasn't there a game of Scrabble in the confessional?"

Kenny reached for it, "I'm game if you are!"

They both selected their letters from the little velvet bag. Caz picked her seven letters and laid them one by one on the plastic rack. She studied them for a short time.

"R G A D N A M" she slowly rearranged the letters to reveal the word **Grandma**, that's a good one, she thought. She was just about to lay the tiles on the board, when the sound of twigs snapping in the forest below made the pair jump, and Caz gasped. "*What was that Kenny!?*"

"Probably just a wild animal, you know, a fox or something."

Caz gazed down at the letters again and laid them on the board. To her astonishment she then heard the peculiar soft humming again, which slowly turned into the sweet melody she had heard earlier that day. "You hear that, Kenny?" she asked.

"What? It was just a fox."

While Kenny deliberated over his letter choice, Caz retrieved her replacement letters, she pulled out the new tiles and placed them on the rack.

F I N D M E - *find me!* This was really getting freaky. 'Grandma', and 'find me' - what were the chances of those words coming up?!

Caz inhaled sharply, "I'm sorry", she said, "I need to pee," Caz didn't really need to pee, but she had a compelling urge to follow the beautiful singing that she had begun to hear, and after all, the game seemed to be telling her to find someone, but who, and what did her Grandma have to do with it, and *how* was it possible a game of Scrabble was trying to communicate with her!? "I'll be back in a minute,"

Kenny threw his hoodie at her, "Here, take this, it's chilly now."

The treehouse creaked and swayed; it was the most unsettling sound.

"You'll be ok?"

"Of course," she smiled.

As she walked down the fluted walkway, Kenny reached over for the kitchen knife he cut the cake with. Something didn't sit easy with him. *Just in case*, he thought.

Caz had reached the forest ground, and to her horror she was still surrounded by the beautiful singing. She began to regret not having brought her torch. She suddenly felt rather dizzy but decided to blame it on the gin rather than anything menacing. She slumped herself down beside a nearby tree stump, and the world began to spin around her. Then, looking up into the trees above could not believe what she saw. The entire canopy of the woodland was glistening with gorgeous white lights. It was like

Christmas. She smiled an intoxicated smile, not knowing if this was the effect of the alcohol, or something else altogether. Now, her whole body began to spin, faster and faster. She held her knees up to her chest and submerged herself in the strange phenomenon. She half wanted to stay there, and half wanted to escape.

Yet above the soft singing she could now make out something else... *it was a whistle*! Three short whistles! *Kenny*! She suddenly awoke from the strange enchantment, and very clearly heard the signal. She returned the whistles, jumped up from the floor, and ran as fast as she could back to the treehouse.

"Caz, are you okay!? You were ages!" Kenny exclaimed. He had been ever so concerned when Caz had not initially returned his whistles.

"Yes, yes I'm ok," she wobbled over to him, and sat on his lap wrapping her arms around him, "I've just had too much to drink, shall we go to bed?"

They agreed that it was probably sensible, it was approaching midnight and it had been an exceptionally long day.

"What about cleaning our teeth?" Kenny asked.

"I'm not going down there again tonight, Kenny!"

They climbed into the sleeping pod, the mattress was surprisingly soft and overall, very cosy indeed. Caz's only complaint was that every time Kenny turned around the whole thing wobbled, but apart from that it was comfortable enough.

They cuddled tightly, and Kenny soon fell asleep. Caz lay there, trying to relax. She concentrated on her breathing. *In through your nose, out through your mouth*, she recited in her mind over and over again. She was beginning to settle, and slowly drifted off. That was before she heard it. *Scratch, scratch, scratch* it went, and it sounded like it was *just* outside the pod. Caz froze. Kenny snored, and she shoved him in an attempt to shut him up. (He didn't wake but the snoring stopped). Caz covered her head with the duvet and didn't move a muscle.   She longed for morning to arrive, and she thought with conviction to herself that if they were lucky enough to make it through the night, they may well have to consider checking out early!

FREYA FRAMPTON

Morning *did* arrive, and it was beautiful to wake up in the trees. Kenny and Caz felt refreshed, and the cool early morning air was invigorating. Kenny stroked Caz's hair; he had always loved her beautiful long hair, it reminded him of Rapunzel from the fairy tales his little sister used to read. Caz was certainly unique, and Kenny loved her very much. He rolled over to face her.

"What shall we do today, Caz?"

"It's going to be another scorcher, but I think we should get out for a walk, are you up for that?"

The treehouse was located within a plantation close to a military firing range and there was a perimeter road which ran around it. They planned to take a walk around it, and perhaps they'd stop at a nearby village for an ice lolly or a drink.

They were soon ready to go. Kenny carried a rucksack with some water and snacks. They made their way up through the forest and after a troublesome patch of nettles, they soon came out into a golden field of corn. The sun was blazing, and the sky was the most dazzling shade of blue. They took on some water before carrying along the path adjacent to the field.

"Cor, it's hot already isn't it!" Kenny remarked. Caz nodded and lifted her sweaty top away from her skin and they stopped again to rest for a moment. "Sure is!" she paused, "Kenny, I know you weren't too keen about staying here, if you want to, we can leave later today rather than staying for the final night?"

"No way! Honestly, I told you last night, this is a great adventure! I *know*, it's a little strange being out in the woods in a treehouse, but it's such an experience. I appreciate you getting this for me, and I *want* to stay tonight, in fact, I could probably get used to staying here for a lot longer than two nights!"

Caz shifted from side to side, unsure what to say. It wasn't the response she was hoping for. She still felt uncomfortable recalling the strange sensations she experienced the night before but forced herself to put it down to the booze. Yet what about the rest of it? The strange singing and Kenny's vivid dream? Well, it had been *very* hot and it was a well-known fact that sun stroke could lead to hallucinations… that would be a logical explanation, and one that Caz could work with.

"Okay, that's cool, I just wanted to check."

They continued their journey and after a few hundred metres they reached the chalky perimeter road. Caz gasped, "Wow, this looks like a road to nowhere if ever I saw one." In front of them lay the bypass stretching out across the landscape for miles and miles. Miraculously, Kenny was able to pick up some signal on his phone to look at the GPS.

"Looking at the map, if we carry on here for around three miles there'll be a left turn that will lead us down to the village," he concurred.

"*There better be a pub in that village*, I'm dying for a nice cold drink!" Chortled Caz.

"Hair of the dog?"

She shook her head. "*No Sir!*"

They relentlessly marched along the white stony road. It was eerie and everlasting as it snaked across the edge of the firing range. The occasional sign clung to the fence to remind them that they were indeed on the perimeter of a military firing range, which Caz found rather unnerving, while Kenny took photos of them. "**DANGER, Unexploded military debris, DO NOT LEAVE THE BYWAY**" or "**DANGER, do not touch any military debris, it may explode and kill you**". She shuddered, what an interesting place to come for a walk, she thought. As they progressed, Kenny noticed that every now and then Caz would look behind her shoulder.

"What's the matter?" he asked.

She sighed, "I'm not sure, it just feels...." she paused, "kind of isolated up here".

Checking his GPS again, Kenny was pleased to inform her that they were advancing well and would hopefully reach the village within the hour. He tried to reassure Caz that it wouldn't be long, and if she could just *try* to enjoy the expedition, she *would* be rewarded at the end. With little choice Caz dragged her feet through the dusty path then suddenly, she stopped.

"*What was that*!?" she swallowed.

"What?" came Kenny's reply.

"I heard something, *something* behind us!"

Kenny turned around, scanning the surrounding countryside, "I didn't hear anything Caz," he reassured her, "I think your imagination is going wild. In fact, you've been *really* edgy ever since we got here."

"I heard *something,*" she insisted.

"I'm sure it was just the wind Caz,"

"*What wind Kenny*? It's like thirty degrees today and *not even the slightest breeze!*"

He took Caz's hand, "Come on, that pub is calling my name!"

Despite Kenny's reassurances, the whole way along Caz continued to get the sense that someone was watching them. Sometimes she got the sensation they were being followed, and other times it was just an uneasy feeling that they weren't actually alone. Even the birds of prey that occasionally soared above them seemed to have a sinister motive. She thought back to one of her favourite novels, 'Tess of the D'urbervilles' and how the author, Thomas Hardy had seemingly been unnerved by long winding roads. He so often wrote them into his stories and Caz now understood just why he may have felt that way. Their water was running low, and she was gasping for that ice-cold drink in the local village pub, so when they started to descend into the valley, she was most relieved, "Ah, at last, civilisation!" She muttered, under her breath.

To their delight there were two pubs to choose from. "The Leaping Gazelle" was the pub of choice, and they were greeted by a very friendly landlady and landlord.

"Good afternoon, lovelies! What can I get you?" The lady was jolly and in good spirits, "Gorgeous day isn't it!" she beamed.

"Cor, yeah," replied Kenny, "it ain't half lovely, but very hot and we're dying for a cold drink. A cider for me please, and Caz?"

"Oh, a pint of diet coke please, and ice!"

The landlady smiled, "Coming right up! I've not seen you two in here before, not from around here?"

"No, we're not, we're on a short holiday, actually," said Caz.

"Ah lovely! Beautiful part of the world, this is. Where are you staying, sweet?" the landlady asked whilst filing the class with Coke.

Caz continued, "Oh, well, we're actually staying in a most unusual place, it's a treehouse in the woods!"

The landlady let go of the glass, and it shattered all over the floor. "Oh! Oh dear! Oh, I'm sorry, *PETE*! Give me a hand over here, will ya?!" then turning to the pair, her tone low and serious, "Are you saying, you're staying in the *treehouse*?!"

The pair slowly nodded, while the landlady continued to stare at them with a dropped jaw.

"Is…is there a problem with that?" stuttered Kenny.

At that moment Pete came over, "Ah, what's happened over here then, did you have one of your funny turns my love?" He began mopping up the mess she had made. "You get the nice lady another drink, my love,"

Turning his attention to Caz and Kenny he apologised, "This one's on the house, so sorry about my wife, she's, uh, well," he lowered his voice to a whisper as the landlady went to fetch more ice, "she can be a bit *fragile* sometimes,"

Caz and Kenny smiled politely, and the landlord went on, "So where did you say you were staying?"

"Oh, you won't believe it, it's an incredible treehouse!" Kenny explained enthusiastically.

The landlord gasped, his hand started shaking, but he managed to steady himself against the bar and didn't drop the glass he was holding.

"The *Treehouse,*" he repeated, drawing a deep breath in, "Well, well, I didn't know they were still renting that place out…"

Caz and Kenny exchanged worried looks, and then returned their focus to Pete.

"Why? What's wrong with the treehouse?" asked Kenny.

"Well, I guess it was a long time ago…"

"*What was a long time ago*?!" said Kenny and Caz in unison.

"You mean, you don't know?" the landlord sounded surprised.

"*Know what*?!" they said again simultaneously.

"I see, you don't know. Well, like I said, it was a *long* time ago, but mark my word, there's been some strange goings on in those woods over the years, not least to mention the disappearance of that poor young lamb, Freya Frampton,"

Caz and Kenny's eyes widened; *they hadn't mentioned any such disappearance in the brochure online...* thought Caz. They encouraged the landlord to continue with his story.

"Freya was in her early twenties. She was the kind of girl that liked the great outdoors and she was always up for an adventure," He stopped himself for a moment, "Let's just say that she came to a rather grizzly end in those woods, I wouldn't like to go into more detail, let's just say, well, there wasn't much of her left when she was eventually found."

Pete was met by the silence of his two dumbfounded guests, and realising how stunned they were, he made an attempt to backtrack, "Oh, I'm sorry, I didn't wanna put you off your stay, I just, I just thought you would have known, like I said, was a *long time ago.*"

At that moment, the landlady came bustling back into the bar with a small bucket of ice under her arm, "Alright then! Now that's all taken care of," she pulled Kenny's cider and poured Caz's coke. "Here you are, my sweets, you enjoy that there now."

Caz and Kenny did not move. They were still processing the gruesome story about the girl in the woods and imagining what on earth had happened to Freya Frampton?

"Did..., did Freya stay *in* the Treehouse?" Caz asked with a small voice. The landlord nodded. The landlady playfully flicked her husband's arm with a bar towel, "Oh, you're not scaring them are you! Must admit, did give me a fright when they said, but it was a long time ago. Now listen, you can go and enjoy those drinks anywhere you like, there's some shade out the back, if you prefer."

Caz and Kenny went into the rear garden where they were gratefully relieved from the blazing afternoon sun. The drinks were refreshing but Caz did wonder whether she should have had something stronger after all.

"What was all that about, Kenny?" Caz took a long slurp of her drink and then held the glass up to her forehead to help her cool down. Kenny scratched his head.

"Let's google it, I'd never heard of any of that stuff before," They both picked up their mobile phones to investigate further. They searched and searched on the internet but failed to find a single article about a young girl called Freya associated with Huntsford Copse. Kenny shielded his mouth with his hand and leant over to Caz, "They were a bit weird Caz, I'd take it *all* with a pinch of salt."

Tessy Braun

A SQUARE OF DARK CHOCOLATE

It was six o clock and Caz and Kenny were finally back at the treehouse. They were hot and bothered from their outing, so before doing anything else they both enjoyed an alfresco bucket-shower before settling down for the evening. The menu consisted of spaghetti bolognaise, followed by some Haribo sweets and chocolate which they looked forward to indulging in. Like the night before, they watched the sunset from the field at the foot of the forest, but this time Caz kept to Pepsi Max. (she still felt a little off colour from the alcohol consumed the night before. Kenny was on the ciders again though).

They sat arm in arm by the firepit as twilight came.

"You know, I could really get used to being here, Caz," he nuzzled into her shoulder. She was shocked how his opinion of the treehouse had turned around, considering his initial preconceptions of the place.

"Really?!" she squeezed his hand.

"*Yes*, it's been great to go back to basics, you've made me realise perhaps I really am wild at heart!" They hugged; it was certainly a trip that they would remember for an awfully long time. The temperature had dipped, and a breeze had picked up. Once again, they thought it would be cosier up in the trees rather than down at ground level. Hand in hand they trudged up the slope, making their way passed the strange post with its peculiar chain, and then to the fluted walkway which led up to their humble abode for the night.

Kenny lit the candles and Caz tore open the sweeties and broke the chocolate into squares (it was the dark variety, Kenny's favourite). They chatted for a while

31

about nothing in particular, before the conversation ran dry, and they were met by the natural sounds of the night. The treehouse creaked, the leaves rustled, and then, they heard twigs snapping below. Caz shrieked "What's that! Not again!" she shuddered. *It was probably a fox or something*, she thought. Kenny squeezed her hand, "We're out in the forest Caz, there's *going* to be noises like this, we're not alone out here, but it's nothing to worry about."

But Caz *was* worried. She couldn't stop thinking about the random letters spelling out **'Grandma'** and **'Find me'**, the strange story that the landlady and landlord had mentioned, not to mention the strange singing, and the lights. It was all way too much to put down to 'sun stroke', there was something else going on here, *she just knew it*, she only wished she knew what on earth it was.

"I'm just going to take a pee, Caz, I'll be back in just a second."

While Kenny was gone Caz reached for the little velvet bag from the game of Scrabble that was still on the table. She shook the letters and then took some out one by one, laying them on the table in front of her.

M A E N O F E J T Y E

Hmmmmmm, she searched for meaning in the letters but there were no anagrams to be found that meant anything at all. *See* she told herself, it was ALL a coincidence, nothing more nothing less. She grabbed a handful of Haribo sweets and stuffed them in her mouth, they were delicious, (her favourite were the little cushioned hearts) and it wasn't long before Kenny was back.

"How about a game of Scrabble?" he suggested.

"No!" she replied sternly, "*No* Scrabble!".

Kenny reached for a square of chocolate, "You know, Caz, after we're back from here, I'm going to treat us to a weekend away in a spa, we can have our own private hot tub, I think you're going to need a weekend away to get over the stress of *this* weekend!"

She smiled at him, he was so thoughtful, and she looked forward to a bright future with him. They sat in silence for a moment, "Kenny?" said Caz.

"Yeah?".

"You didn't hear anything strange down there when you went for a pee, did you?"

"Nothing, nothing at all".

She smiled again, trying to calm herself, but regardless she was starting to feel anxious. "That's good".

Kenny pulled his chair closer to hers, and rubbed her knee affectionately, "I love you; you've got nothing to worry about, I'll look after you."

She smiled again; how lucky she was to have him. He was right, she was overreacting.

"I need to go for a pee now, Kenny,"

"Shall I come with you?"

Not wanting to be a burden she declined, "Oh no, I'll be absolutely fine, don't be silly, I'm also gonna pop down to the kitchen, I left the other packet of sweets down there."

As Caz reached the ground level, she suddenly began to feel lightheaded, which was strange, as she hadn't been drinking alcohol that evening. She dismissed the feeling but then suddenly became unstable and ended up slipping on the loose soil sliding down a few yards on her bottom. Kenny heard the commotion and sent three whistles out, and Caz returned them immediately.

Regrettably, she hadn't brought a torch with her, but what she thought were solar lanterns paved the way. *That's funny, I don't recall there being any solar lanterns here*, she thought, but again, she dismissed her concern, becoming increasingly lightheaded and dizzy.

Caz thought she was on route for the kitchen, but her navigation had somewhat failed her for she found herself a fair distance away from the treehouse, and not anywhere near the kitchen. She was disorientated, and most peculiarly she could now make out a faint singing, a melody so beautiful, a melody so familiar. Her eyes became heavy and a feeling of exhaustion overcame her, she slumped down at the foot of a tree stump.

After what seemed like an awfully long time indeed, perhaps even hours, her eyes flickered, and slowly opened. It felt like a bright light was shining directly into them, "*Kenny!*" she called, but no matter how loudly she called, her voice was muffled and weak. She shielded her vision from the brightness with her hand, and as her eyes adjusted to the light, she opened them wider. *What on earth is that!?* She thought. It was ginormous, the size of football. A sphere of bright, white light, flickering and hovering in the air just a few metres away!

It was alluring and was indeed the most beautiful thing she had ever seen, and if she was hearing coherently, the singing was coming from within the orb of light itself. Trembling, she stepped towards the light, holding her hand out as if she were going to touch it.

***

Up on the deck, Kenny was getting restless, she'd taken over ten minutes now, it didn't take *that* long to go down to the kitchen to grab the sweeties and have a pee. He sounded another three short whistles, and awaited Caz's reply, but this time, no whistles came back. Kenny sighed, he would have to go and look for her if she wasn't back soon. He shone his torch around the platform, not looking for anything in particular, but noticed some markings in the wooden panels by the confessional. *"I didn't spot them before, how strange"* he thought, moving closer to the carvings he traced his fingers in the grooves. A beast, of some sort, and what was this next to it? Some sort of angel. That's interesting, I wonder who carved them, he thought.

***

Caz was now within hand reach of the mysterious ball of light. She was just about to make contact with it when she stopped abruptly and studied the light with intensity. Its appearance began to change right in front of her eyes. Its shape was shifting from a flickering fire ball, into something quite different altogether. She saw a face, a body, and a hand reaching out and beckoning her to follow it. Its form was so familiar, and it was then that a memory was triggered. "*Grandma*?!" she whispered, "Are you there?" The 'thing' in front of her was not her grandma though, it was much younger than her in looks, but Caz did now remember the old stories much more clearly. She began to realise what it was she had come face to face with. *Well of course!* It could be nothing else. It simply must have been *the Tree Nymph*, otherwise known as one of the Great Tree Spirits of the English Woodlands. This particular Tree Spirit appeared to be the very one that grandma had told her about in the stories all those years ago, and no doubt the very one that Kenny had seen when he thought he was dreaming the day before.

Caz had always felt a calling to the woodland, and her grandma had once told her she was very special, (and brave). It all made sense now. This whole weekend away had been her *calling*, her *Life's Mission*. This was surely the very reason she recognised the woodland and had such an intense feeling of Deja vu. The story was now all coming back to her. As she approached the Tree Nymph, a foreboding feeling came upon her as she also remembered about the dog in the story, or was it a wolf? The Wolf with red eyes, *yes that was it*. In the story, the Tree Nymph had captured the wolf, and tied it to a post in the forest so it couldn't stop her from taking her victims.

Caz had a flash back to the moment she and Kenny had found the post with the chain that led to nothing, and she began to piece the story together, *had the Wolf escaped?*

***

Back at the treehouse Kenny was becoming agitated. It had now been a good fifteen minutes since Caz had left. Surely it doesn't take *this* long, he thought. He heard a shuffling on the ground below.

"Caz?! Is that you?" he hissed, feeling a little unnerved himself at this point. The forest at night had the ability to alter reality to such a great extent he was now questioning his own logic, and no longer felt safe. A foreboding notion swept over him, and his main concern was that Caz may well be in grave danger.

He fastened a headlamp and adjusted it, so it sat snugly on his head. He clutched the kitchen knife that had been left on the table. "*Caz*?!" he called again, slightly louder, but received no reply. He had no choice but to leave the relative comfort of the treehouse to find her. He gingerly stepped down the fluted walkway, desperately trying to be as quiet as possible, but the walkway creaked too much under foot. Once he had reached the bottom, he circled around, shining his light into the forest in hope to find Caz crouching by the side of a tree, but no such luck befell him. He whistled out again, three short whistles. In return came no whistles. He yelled out into the forest, "CAZ!" but instead of three whistles, a low monstrous growl returned his call. It sounded just like the noise that he had heard in his dream. His breathing quickened. *What the hell was that?* A fox did not sound like that, a fox's cry was more akin to the sound of a baby's cry than a growl. He held the kitchen knife out and with it outstretched, turned side to side, its pathetic blade shining in the slither of moonlight that crept beneath the canopy of trees. He heard movement, but it sounded like it came from all corners of the forest, and he couldn't for the life of him pinpoint it. It came again, this unnatural roar, it was a groan like no other he had heard, and it chilled him to the bone.

Now panting, he flashed his head from side to side. *Where did it come from?* It came again, and this time he was able to associate it with further up in the woods. He *had* to find Caz, he *had* to make sure she was alright, and save her from whatever it was that was out there. He wasn't going to let them die in this forest, that was for sure!

*****

The beautiful figure of the Tree Spirit was now fully formed, and she really was the most beautiful thing that Caz had ever seen in her life. Her long wispy hair was lit up by each individual strand, and she had the most delicate of features. Floating a few inches above the ground, she was most certainly a creature from another dimension.

"Come…come to me, my child," the Nymph held out one hand and led Caz deeper into the woods.

"*Who are you!*" Caz exclaimed but she followed without hesitation, like to follow it, was her destiny.

"It is your path to join me child, to join me within the bark of these trees, to guard these woodlands, forever more," whispered the Tree Nymph in her melodic voice.

"I know, my Grandma told me, when I was little," recalled Caz, thinking back to how obsessed she had been with the stories.

"Yes…you are meant to be here," The Tree Spirit smiled, "Come…" Caz stepped forward and strangely, all sense of fear had been abandoned, instead she had an overwhelming feeling of belonging, and didn't once take the time to think of poor Kenny, let alone her own family at home.

"Your Grandma, she is here too, come," the Nymph sang. *Her Grandma was still alive?* She choked, *what?* Could they really be together again? This was all too much to comprehend. Caz took a few more steps forward, but then they both froze! A monstrous growl filled their ears and reverberated all throughout the forest. It was loud, Caz suspected no more than a few metres away, and a heavy beastly breathing could be heard from all corners of the forest.

The Nymph's eyes glowed, yet now in not such a gentle way. Instead, she was becoming angry and rapidly lost her peaceful and serene appearance. Her flowing hair now shot out in every direction; embers flew out of it which reminded Caz of sparklers on bonfire night.

"The wild dog! He has found me once more," She let out a tortuous wail. *"Come! Quick!"* she hissed, *"Before it is too late!"* she held onto Caz's hand, her sharp nails dug into Caz's palm with such force that her skin was pierced, and blood began to run down her wrists.

TO THE TREES

It was then that out of the shadows the Wolf made his grand appearance. Yet he was like no wolf Caz had ever laid her eyes upon before. Her first observation was his size, he was larger than an average wolf, more muscular and robust. He stood on his two hind legs, like a cross between human and wild dog. His body was illuminated by a bright light, which gave Caz visibility to see his sharp white fangs as he snarled in their direction. He was a monster.

Looking to the Tree Nymph for guidance, Caz trembled, but the Nymph only tugged more sharply at Caz's hand.

"*Come! He will stop you from returning home, stop you from being with your Grandma again,*" The Tree Spirit's light was fading every time the Wolf took a step closer. His very presence seemed to have a diminishing effect on her power and her light. *What was happening? How could any of this actually be reality?* Caz's thoughts ran through her head at a million miles per hour, no longer was she feeling seduced by the Tree Spirit, in fact she was feeling more compos mentis every second. "*Kenny! Kenny! Help, Help!*" she screamed, and she whistled and whistled like a madwoman, in desperation to attract his attention.

In that instance something, or *someone* pounced on the Wolf, halting him in his tracks towards Caz. It let out a howl, and arched it's back up revealing it's matted blood-stained undercoat.

"*It's okay Caz! I'm here*! I need you to *run!*" It was Kenny! It was *her* Kenny, and he was *here*, and he was going to save them both so they could go home and live happily ever after.

Yet it was far from over. Kenny stabbed the wolf, again and again and again, hoping that he could stop the hideous beast from reaching Caz, if only just for enough time to allow her to flee. Though the Wolf was strong, (much stronger than Kenny and his kitchen knife), Kenny was confident it would buy enough time for Caz to make her escape.

The Tree Nymph laughed, "He has come to save you!" she purred, "how sweet he is, yet he knows not, that he is letting you go instead! He has released you to the trees, *forever!*" The Nymph morphed into the tree directly behind her, and with her grip so tight on Caz's hand she pulled and pulled, dragging Caz into the bark of the tree too. As Caz slipped backwards into the tree, she held her arms out as if she were one crucified, as the tree nymph now pulled her by her long straw-coloured hair.

"*No!*" quite broken from the Nymph's strange spell. "*No!*" she bellowed as loud as she could into the forest, but her voice could not travel far enough, and she sunk right into that tree.

It was all too late. As Kenny had tried to save her from the Wolf, unbeknown to him, he had allowed the Tree Nymph to take her, and once taken by a Tree Nymph there is *never ever* any going back…

TIME TO GO HOME

Kenny slumped to the ground; his energy entirely depleted. He no longer had the momentum to wrestle with the Wolf. It was fair to say, however, that he had put up a good fight, (taking into consideration his feeble weapon). In Kenny's favour, he had succeeded in injuring the creature, for purple blood could be seen dripping from its superficial wounds. Sadly, they were no more than superficial, and now the Wolf was *furious*!

He turned to face his helpless victim drooling uncontrollably, his saliva was thick and gloopy. He snarled at poor defenceless Kenny, then shook his head and drool flicked all over Kenny's face. It was utterly repulsive, but Kenny was no longer at an advantage, and could do nothing to overcome the beast. He did try to kick, in an attempt to escape, but the with ease the Wolf merely scooped him up with one arm and threw him over his shoulder. He set off towards the treehouse, stopping just before they got there, by the ominous metal post.

It was really rather strange what happened next as his eyes began to glow red. He dropped Kenny on his back, and stood over him, still growling and snarling. Kenny cowered into a pathetic heap, as the beast then used the chains to tie him securely to the post.

"Please! No! Let me go!" he wailed, as if the Wolf would have any pity for him with his woeful begging. He then omitted a strange light from his red eyes which shone all around Kenny's body creating a channel of light between the two of them. *What the hell was going on?* Thought Kenny, his pulse was racing. The most peculiar thing was yet to transpire; the Landlord *did* mention that strange things had happened in these woods, so it would be no surprise to hear that the Wolf began to painstakingly draw energy through the channel of light. Ever so slowly, little by little, the Wolf began to resemble Kenny.

Poor Kenny let out a deep groan and then held his chained hands out in front of him. Yet they were not hands. He howled as he came to realise that *he now was the Wolf.* He let out a final harrowing bay and tugged violently at the chain that fastened him to the post.

The Wolf, now assuming Kenny's form, brushed himself off and straightened his clothing. He tore the headlamp from Kenny's head, and left him whimpering in the darkness. Clearing his throat and brushing back his hair he muttered.

"*It's time to go home...*" before running off towards the nearby village.

ABOUT THE AUTHOR

Tessy is a mother of two lively young boys and enjoys an active lifestyle with them. While originally from West Devon, Tessy now lives in Bristol, in the United Kingdom.

In addition to writing Tessy enjoys exploring the countryside and playing the violin and the cello. Tessy has been writing poetry and stories throughout her whole life but has only been publishing her work since 2018.

Please check out the author's other publications on Amazon, if you enjoyed this short story you may like the narrative poem "In the Little Woodland Clearing" and "The Midnight Masquerade".

Tessy would be extremely grateful if you would spare the time to leave a review for *The Treehouse* on Amazon.

Printed in Great Britain
by Amazon

23643102R00030